2

Two sturdy feet
showing me the way.

3

Three ripe bananas
ready on a plate.

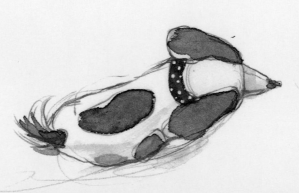

4

Four little wheels
take me to the gate.

5

Five broody hens,
feathers fluffed
with pride.

6

Six fresh eggs.
I think I'll have mine fried.

7

Seven tired friends
sleeping on the floor.

8

Eight juicy apples.
Who could ask for more?

9

Nine bright butterflies
bigger than my hand.

10

Ten red flowers,
where they come to land.

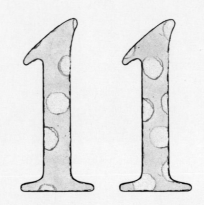

Eleven quiet birds
high up on the wire.

12

Twelve dry sticks
collected for the fire.

Twenty wise owls
on a shelf by the door.

Hundreds

of books

piled up on the floor.

Thousands

of raindrops
falling from the sky.

Millions

of stars to count.
One day I might try.
But …

One silver moon shining big and bright.

One loving kiss, now I'm tucked in tight.

Good night!